DOCTOR DUCK
AND
NURSE SWAN
by Bernard Wiseman

Scholastic Inc.
New York Toronto London Aukland Sydney Tokyo

for Susan, Pete, Mike and Andy—

ISBN 0-590-33628-2

12 11 10 9 8 7 6 5 4 3 2 1   4   5 6 7 8 9/8 0/9

Printed in the U.S.A.   09

"Good morning," said Doctor Duck.
Nurse Swan cried, "You are late!
Look at the CLOCK, Ductor Dock!"

Doctor Duck cried, "My name is not Ductor Dock! It is Doctor Ductor. No— I mean Doctor Dock! No! No!"

Nurse Swan said, "Oh, we must get
to work. Mister Eagle, please come in."

"Doctor," said Mister Eagle, "I am BALD!"
Doctor Duck said, "You are SUPPOSED to be. You are a BALD Eagle."

"Yes," cried Mister Eagle. "I am a BALD
Eagle, but I want HAIR. I want a MOP of hair!"
Doctor Duck said, "I can't give you a MOP
of hair, but..."

"...here is a HAIR of MOP!"

Nurse Swan said, "Mister Catfish is next."
"Doctor," cried Mister Catfish, "I am a
CATfish, but I can't MEOW!"

Doctor Duck said, "Catfish are not SUPPOSED to meow."

Mister Catfish asked, "What should catfish SAY?"

Doctor Duck cried, "I DON'T KNOW!"

"I DON'T KNOW! I DON'T KNOW!
I DON'T KNOW!"

Nurse Swan said, "Mister Turkey is next."
"Doctor," said Mister Turkey, "I bump
into things."

"Well," said Doctor Duck, "take off your hat.
Then you will see where you are going."

"No! No!" cried Mister Turkey. "Then
everyone would see that I am a TURKEY!
And Thanksgiving is coming soon."

Doctor Duck said, "I will have to OPERATE!"

"I CAN SEE! I CAN SEE!"

"Miss Sheep is next," said Nurse Swan.
Miss Sheep said, "Doctor, I feel too WARM."

Doctor Duck said, "Hold this in your mouth."

"Well," said Doctor Duck, "you are NOT SICK.
I will have to OPERATE!"

Miss Sheep cried, "But you said I was NOT
SICK—"

"Yes!" shouted Doctor Duck. "That is why
I MUST OPERATE!"

"Do you FEEL BETTER now?" asked
Doctor Duck.

"No!" cried Miss Sheep. "Now I feel
too COLD!"

"Don't worry," said Doctor Duck. "I know what to do."

"Mister Anteater is next," said Nurse Swan. "Look—" cried Mister Anteater. "My nose is too LONG! Everyone LAUGHS at me."

Doctor Duck said, "I know what to do. Get undressed."

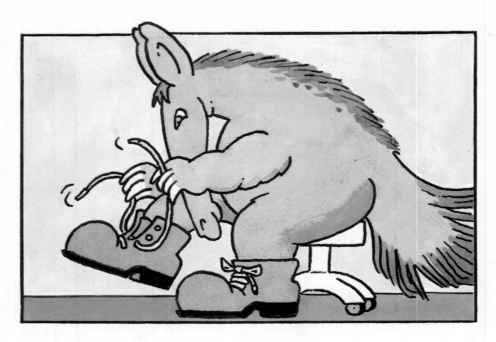

Doctor Duck said, "Go tell everyone
your nose is a LEG!"

"Mister Snake is next," said Nurse Swan.
"Doctor," cried Mister Snake, "I can't catch
a ball. I can't jump rope. No one will PLAY
with me."

"They will!" said Doctor Duck. "Nurse, give me a big Band-Aid—"

"Everyone will play with a HULA-HOOP!"

Nurse Swan yawned. "Oh, it is late—
Doctor Duck, look at the CLUCK!"

"You mean CLOCK," said Doctor Duck.

"Yes," said Nurse Swan. "I mean CLOCK,
Ductor Dock."

Doctor Duck cried, "My name is not DUCTOR
DOCK! My name is DOCTOR DUCTOR! No—
my name is—ohhh—GOOD NIGHT!"